# Tenzin's Deer

The musk deer is a small, shy, solitary animal found throughout the forested regions of Asia and Russia. Musk, the oil base used in a number of perfumes, is one of the world's most expensive natural products; up to five times more expensive than gold. The musk deer is widely poached for its precious scent gland and, as a result, this beautiful creature is facing extinction.

*For Emma, a lover of animals, Gabriel who is so brave, David who fulfills his gifts and for Jack who went back to the wild – B. S.*

*Dedicated to the Musk Deer and to the memory of my human and nonhuman friends who have taken The Journey ahead of me – D. M.*

Barefoot Books
3 Bow Street, 3rd Floor
Cambridge, MA 02138

Text copyright © 2003 by Barbara Soros
Illustrations copyright © 2003 by Danuta Mayer
The moral right of Barbara Soros to be identified as the author and Danuta Mayer to be identified as the illustrator of this work has been asserted
First published in the United States of America in 2003 by Barefoot Books, Inc.

This book is printed on 100% acid-free paper
This book was typeset in Sabon 11.5pt
The illustrations were prepared in gouache on 100% unsized rag paper

Graphic design by designsection, Frome, Somerset
Color separation by Grafiscan, Italy
Printed and bound in China

3 5 7 9 8 6 4

Soros, Barbara.
         Tenzin's Deer / written by Barbara Soros ; illustrated by Danuta Mayer. --1st ed.
[32] p. : col. ill. ;  cm.
Summary: When young Tenzin discovers a wounded musk deer high up in the hills,
he takes it home to try and heal it. Through a dream, Tenzin learns how he can cure
his new friend, and day by day, the deer gets better. But once the deer has recovered,
Tenzin must learn the most important lesson of all: to love enough to let the deer go.
ISBN 1 9 0 5 2 3 6 5 7 3
1. Musk deer – Juvenile fiction.
2. Deer – Juvenile fiction.
3. Wildlife rescue – Juvenile fiction.
(1. Musk deer – Fiction.
2. Deer – Fiction.
3. Wildlife rescue – Fiction.)
I. Mayer, Danuta. II. Title.

[E]   2003

# Tenzin's Deer

To
Kevin Tenzin Fosco Perry,
May you be safe from
harm. May you love others well.
May you be kind to all the creatures
of the earth. And may you love this
book as much as I do. You truly are
a treasure.
Love, Light + Magic,
Traci

*written by* **Barbara Soros** *illustrated by* **Danuta Mayer**

**Barefoot Books**
*Celebrating Art and Story*

In old Tibet, horses ran free over wide, open plains. The land was watered by melting snows and protected from fierce winds by the high Himalayan mountains. Under a great big sky, people once lived peacefully together, in villages and in houses made of roughly-hewn stones.

At dawn, women stood on their rooftops burning juniper branches on charcoal fires. They offered dried fruit or yak butter to the gods and protective spirits of the mountains. The wisps of smoke carried the sweet smells of the juniper and the sweet sounds of the prayers high into the sky.

"May no harm come to us. May we love one another well. May we be kind to all creatures of the earth," they prayed as the sun rose and warmed the valley.

In one of these houses lived a boy who was born just as a comet traveled the heavens. Everyone agreed that he was like a brilliant light in the night sky. Throughout the village, he was known for his tender and loving heart. He was wiser than his young years and was born with the knowledge of many generations in his memory, and so he was called Tenzin, Holder of the Teachings.

Tenzin was kind to old people, to sick people and to animals both wild and tame. He knew how to speak to the giant hairy yaks and dzogs, and with only his voice he could lead them from pasture to pasture. He knew how to gain the trust of the great mastiffs that guarded the villages at night. When he approached them, they rolled on their backs like pussycats, and he rubbed their bellies.

Tenzin wandered the hills, listening to the songs of the birds and learning how to sing them himself. He followed the tracks of foxes, until he found their homes and surprised them. He did not harm them, he just liked to watch them, and sing to them and sometimes bring them some treats. He had been taught that everything on the earth is alive and has a soul — even the rocks, the trees, the stars in the heavens. For the Tibetan people, everyone and everything is sister and brother.

One day, Tenzin followed the tracks of a musk deer. He noticed that they looked heavy and slow, rather than light and fast, as they sank into the earth instead of sitting on the surface. Finally, he found the tiny, young deer with her large ears and soft brown coat. She lay on her side in a pool of blood and cried from deep inside.

"Help me, I am in pain."

A hunter's arrow had lodged in the deer's breast. Tenzin knew that if he pulled it out, the arrowhead would rip the muscle and tear the animal's heart. So instead he closed his eyes and slowed his breath, saying quietly to the deer, "May no harm come to you. May you soon be free from pain. May your suffering stop." He felt the pain of the deer as if it was his own pain, and he felt the fear of the deer as if it was his own fear. Then he saw in his mind the deer without the arrow in her chest, free from pain, but he did not know how this would happen.

"What shall I do now?" Tenzin asked into the air. Gently the deer responded, "Carry me from here and do nothing now. It will come to you in a dream."

Tenderly, Tenzin carried the deer to his house and made a bed
for her on the roof with hay and cloth. As he lay her down he
whispered to her, "I will name you Jampa, Loving Kindness."
Jampa opened and closed her soulful eyes several times, as if
agreeing to her new name.

At night, Tenzin lay down next to Jampa and fell asleep with his
arm gently around her shoulder. And while the stars twinkled
above them and the moon stood watch in the sky, he had a dream.
In the dream he saw the water of the melting snow rushing down
the mountains, and as it rushed, it loosened stones and red clay
from the earth, which flowed easily with the clear water.

The next morning, as the villagers offered their prayers to the protective spirits, Tenzin carried Jampa through the misty valley into the hills. He walked slowly, tenderly repeating, "May no harm come to you. May you be free from pain." He walked and prayed until he reached a stream. Laying the deer in the stream, he held her with care, so the clear water could wash her wound. Jampa winced, and made little moaning sounds, but she lay still, letting the boy gently hold her as the waters of the stream washed her. Blood ran with the water, and as it did, the arrow loosened on its own and Tenzin was able to remove it with ease.

Jampa looked at Tenzin with her tender, brown eyes and gratefully said, "Thank you, may many blessings come into your life."

A hole was left in the side of the deer. The boy asked, "What shall I do now?"

"Do nothing now, it will come to you in a dream," Jampa responded.

That night on the roof, Tenzin lay with his arm around his new friend, gazing out at the black sky with millions of twinkling stars. Before long he fell asleep. As he slept he dreamed of the beautiful myrobalan plant with its flowers and leaves. In his dream there was a hole in the earth, and when he placed the myrobalan plant on top, the hole closed and the bare earth reseeded itself and grasses began to grow.

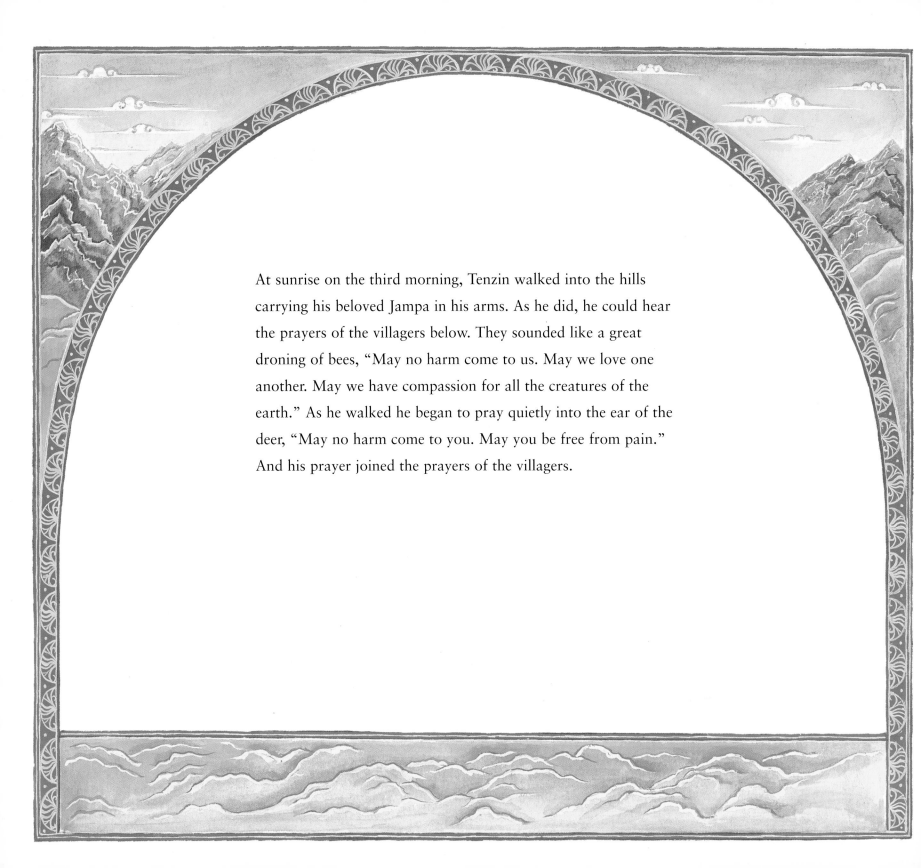

At sunrise on the third morning, Tenzin walked into the hills carrying his beloved Jampa in his arms. As he did, he could hear the prayers of the villagers below. They sounded like a great droning of bees, "May no harm come to us. May we love one another. May we have compassion for all the creatures of the earth." As he walked he began to pray quietly into the ear of the deer, "May no harm come to you. May you be free from pain." And his prayer joined the prayers of the villagers.

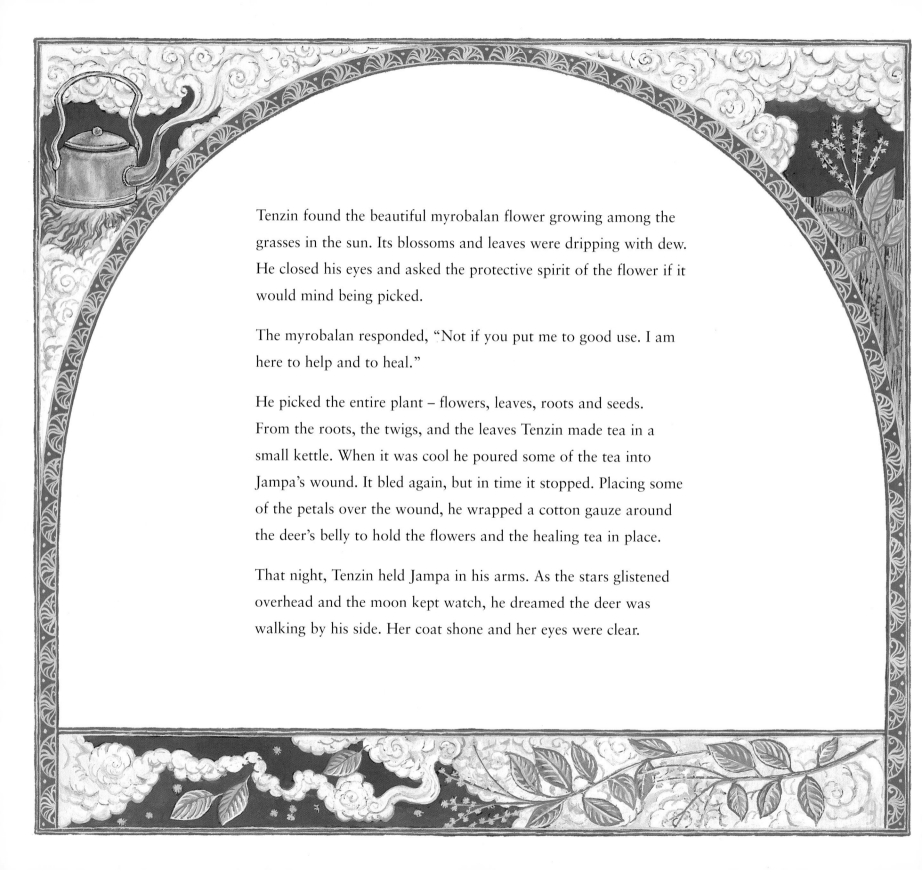

Tenzin found the beautiful myrobalan flower growing among the grasses in the sun. Its blossoms and leaves were dripping with dew. He closed his eyes and asked the protective spirit of the flower if it would mind being picked.

The myrobalan responded, "Not if you put me to good use. I am here to help and to heal."

He picked the entire plant – flowers, leaves, roots and seeds. From the roots, the twigs, and the leaves Tenzin made tea in a small kettle. When it was cool he poured some of the tea into Jampa's wound. It bled again, but in time it stopped. Placing some of the petals over the wound, he wrapped a cotton gauze around the deer's belly to hold the flowers and the healing tea in place.

That night, Tenzin held Jampa in his arms. As the stars glistened overhead and the moon kept watch, he dreamed the deer was walking by his side. Her coat shone and her eyes were clear.

The days moved on. Each day Tenzin cleaned the wound with fresh
tea from the myrobalan plant. Soon the deer stood on her legs,
though she was still fragile. Often, they sat peacefully on a hillside,
Jampa resting in Tenzin's lap as he stroked her delicate head. During
these times, Tenzin prayed. "May no harm come to you. May you
be at peace. May my breath enter your body, may my strength be
your strength. And may your eyes be deep like the sea, your heart
be strong like a mountain and your mind be free like the sky."

Jampa grew stronger and soon she and Tenzin were seen everywhere
together: by the river where the women washed their clothes, or
walking with herds of dzogs that the villagers milked daily for
butter and milk. Tenzin and Jampa played by the stupas where
people gathered to pray, and by the edge of the monastery where
monks studied and lived together.

More than anything, Tenzin loved his deer. They slept together, ate
together, listened to the wind together and spent many nights gazing
at the changing moon over the vast mountains.

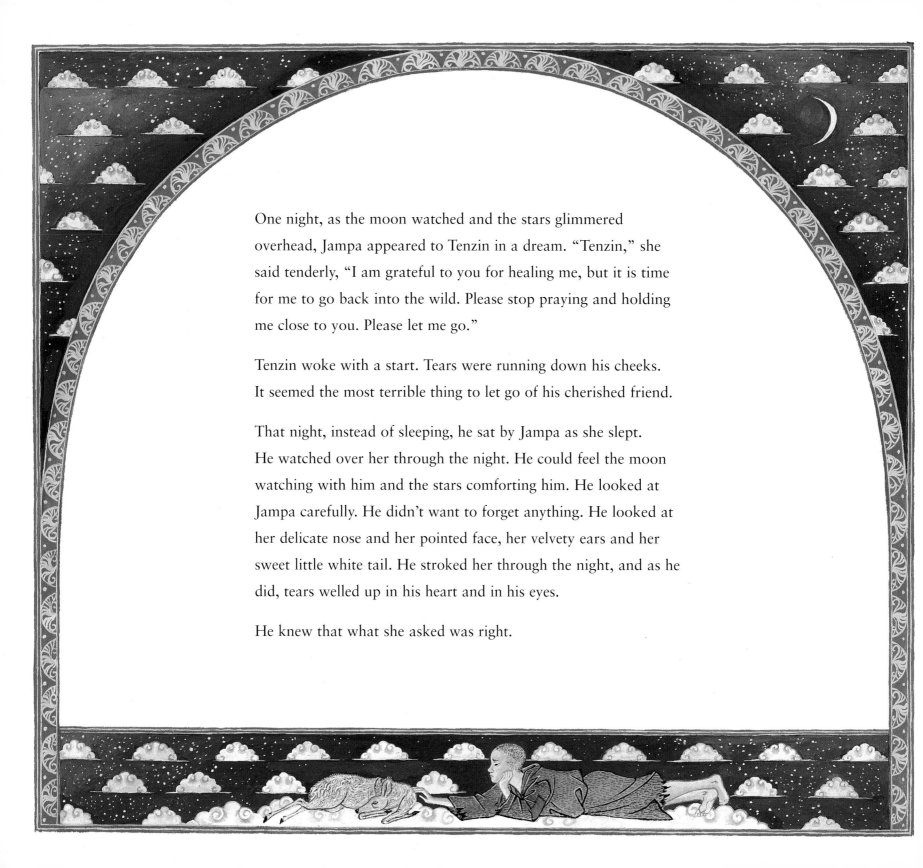

One night, as the moon watched and the stars glimmered overhead, Jampa appeared to Tenzin in a dream. "Tenzin," she said tenderly, "I am grateful to you for healing me, but it is time for me to go back into the wild. Please stop praying and holding me close to you. Please let me go."

Tenzin woke with a start. Tears were running down his cheeks. It seemed the most terrible thing to let go of his cherished friend.

That night, instead of sleeping, he sat by Jampa as she slept. He watched over her through the night. He could feel the moon watching with him and the stars comforting him. He looked at Jampa carefully. He didn't want to forget anything. He looked at her delicate nose and her pointed face, her velvety ears and her sweet little white tail. He stroked her through the night, and as he did, tears welled up in his heart and in his eyes.

He knew that what she asked was right.

And just at the time when night begins to meet dawn, when the veil between dream and day is at its thinnest, Tenzin reached into his heart, as deeply as the arrow which struck the deer, to summon all of his courage. At the moment he felt his very bravest, he began to breathe with Jampa. As she breathed in, he breathed in. As she breathed out, he breathed out. His breath deepened, and he felt as if he was now breathing for her, making it easier for her to leave. He said gently, "Go, beloved friend, to the wild. Do not be held by my love. Go bravely and well and clearly know we will meet again. Return to the earth as a gift."

Almost as soon as he uttered the last word, Jampa sprang to her feet and was gone. Tenzin felt strange at first, as though some part of himself had disappeared. His belly felt hollow and he wanted to cry. Slowly, dragging his feet, he walked to the top of the mountain just as the first rays of the sun hit the hills. As the prayers of the villagers echoed through the valley he looked out, remembering all the places he had walked with Jampa.

In his mind, Tenzin imagined Jampa leaping through the hills. He could feel her joy as if it were his own joy, and he could feel her freedom as if it were his own freedom. Overhead, a great winged eagle swirled in front of the sun. Below, swans glided onto a lake. Tenzin could hear Jampa's melodious voice coming from far off. "Thank you, Tenzin. Thank you. I will remember. When you need me, I will come to you."

And that is what happened. As Tenzin grew into a man he became a very fine doctor, tending with great care to the sick people in his village. Often, he used the sacred myrobalan plant. He was a devoted husband and father who taught his children to be loving and kind.

Sometimes Jampa came to Tenzin in his dreams. She was radiant, strong and all grown up. She would say to him as he had said to her, "May no harm come to you. May you be at peace. And may your eyes be deep like the sea, your heart be solid like a mountain and your mind be free like the sky."

# Afterword

This is a story about the power of compassion, the guidance of dreams, the gift of healing and the ability to love deeply and to let go. Tenzin knows that every living thing, animate and inanimate, should be treated with respect. He knows how to wish others well. He knows how to ask questions, how to listen to his intuition, how to honor a dream, how to be brave and generous in the face of loss.

Tenzin's knowledge is not only his own. Like his name, it belongs to an emotionally and spiritually mature culture whose people value gentleness and sensitivity over aggression. The Tibetan people have used prayer and meditative practices for generations, not only to honor the spirits of the land and the heavens, but to hone their hearts, like finely polished jewels. The practice of Loving Kindness, which their morning prayers mirror and Tenzin's words and actions reflect, has been recited throughout Tibet for nearly thirteen hundred years.

The myrobalan plant is the all-healing plant, and is a symbol of the rich complexity and wholeness of the ancient Tibetan medical tradition. To be a doctor is an honored role in Tibetan society and is considered a spiritual calling. The doctor lives a life of integrity and compassion, a life of inner and outer balance. The medicine the doctor practices addresses the body, mind and spirit. Loving Kindness is a foundation practice of the medical tradition as well.

In Buddhism, non-attachment is another key practice that frees us from suffering. In the story, Tenzin uses all of his understanding to let the deer go. He struggles to practice non-attachment. This is difficult enough for an adult to understand; it is even more difficult for a child. But children must learn from early on to let go. They must learn to let go of a friend or a relative who moves away; to let go of the configuration of a family where there is a divorce or a loved one dies; or to surrender a hope that is lost, or a dream that cannot be fulfilled.

Children, like all of us, must learn to love deeply, to wish others well and then to let nature or destiny fulfill its role. Often when we let go there are gifts. When we let go with grace and bravery, often the love we feel deepens and returns to us in unexpected ways.

Tenzin's dreams and actions foreshadow his future vocation as a healer. In most cultures it is common for a child's future to show itself symbolically in dreams and in the actions of the child. In Tibetan culture, these signs are overtly acknowledged and honored very early on. In this way there is a natural integration of the conscious with the unconscious mind as the children of each generation are guided toward their destinies.